THE FLYTRAP FILES

By **TOM ANGLEBERGER**
with story consultant Charlie Angleberger

Illustrated by
HEATHER FOX

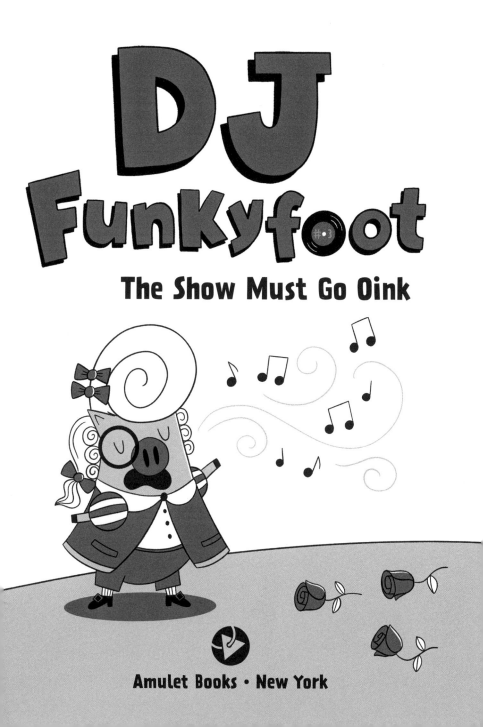

DJ FunKyfoot #3

The Show Must Go Oink

Amulet Books · New York

Cataloging-in-Publication Data has been applied for and may be obtained from the Library of Congress.

ISBN 978-1-4197-4732-8

Text copyright © 2022 Tom Angleberger
Illustrations copyright © 2022 Heather Fox
Book design by Heather Kelly

Printed and bound in U.S.A.
10 9 8 7 6 5 4 3 2 1

Amulet Books are available at special discounts when purchased in quantity for premiums and promotions as well as fundraising or educational use. Special editions can also be created to specification. For details, contact specialsales@abramsbooks.com or the address below.

Amulet Books® is a registered trademark of Harry N. Abrams, Inc.

ABRAMS The Art of Books
195 Broadway, New York, NY 10007
abramsbooks.com

To Heather Fox,
the artist who made
DJ Funkyfoot a star!
—T. A.

CONTENTS

Opening

y phone rang.

"Greetings," I said. "I am DJ Funkyfoot and I am at YOUR service."

"Hello, DJ Funkyfoot," said a cool voice. "I am Krystal Wombat, president of Wombat Jam Records."

I was very excited!

Company presidents are often rich.

And rich people can hire butlers.

And I am a butler!

Since butlers are always very polite, I answered Krystal Wombat as politely as I possibly could.

"Madame Wombat," I said. "It would be my great honor to serve as your butler!"

"Oh, I've already got a butler," she said. "What I need is a hot hip-hop hit record. That's why I'm calling you."

ALAS! This was yet another phone call from someone who thought I was a hip-hop star because of my name, DJ Funky-foot. (Middle name: MC.)

My parents hoped that I would become a hip-hop star. They gave me this name. They made me take hip-hop lessons. They bought me turntables and microphones.

But through it all, I followed a different dream.

The dream of being a butler! Of serving fancy tea and fancy food on fancy dishes in a very fancy way.

Unfortunately, every time someone hires me to be a butler, things don't turn out fancy. They turn out messy—very messy—and I lose the job.

"Well," said Krystal Wombat, with a voice that was a little less cool and a little more impatient. "Do you have a hot hip-hop hit record? Your mother told me you did!"

"My mother?"

"Yes, I ran into her at Cousin Yuk Yuk's Pickle Buffet, and she told me to call you to hear your latest, hottest, hip-hoppest recording."

"I am sorry," I said. "My mom was just bragging. I do not have a recording to play for you."

"I understand," she said. "Moms do that sometimes. But let me know if you ever do have a record to play for me."

"Yes, Madame Wombat," I said. "I certainly will."

PART 1

This Is a Job for Job for Super Butler!

Chapter 1

My phone rang again!

"Greetings," I said. "I am DJ Funkyfoot, and I am—"

Before I could finish, a very deep but very fancy voice grunted at me.

"No, I do not need a DJ. I need a butler. Goodbye."

"Wait!" I shouted. And then I remembered that butlers don't shout. So I said very politely, "Sir, I AM a butler."

"Are you sure?" grunted the very deep but very fancy voice. "To me you sound like a hip-hop star who shouts."

"No, sir," I said. "I am indeed a butler, and I am at your service."

"Hurmmmmmmm," grunted the voice thoughtfully.

Then there was a long awkward pause. Should I say something else? Or should I give him time to think? I was excited about possibly getting a job as a butler, BUT a butler should not get too excited. So I decided to wait.

Finally the voice grunted again.

"I don't need just any butler. I need a butler who can do things EXACTLY the way that I ask. I need the very best butler. Are you the very best butler?"

I thought about my career as a butler so far—the disasters, the messes, the car wrecks. Could I really claim to be the "best" butler? No. But if I didn't claim to be the best butler, I wouldn't get the job. I said the only thing I could.

"I TRY to be the best butler, sir," I said. "And I will TRY to do everything exactly the way you ask."

"EXACTLY?" squealed the voice, which suddenly got very high-pitched.

"Exactly, sir," I said.

"All right. You are hired," grunted the voice, suddenly very low again. "You must be ready at once! We leave the city in one hour for the HooberHustle Music Festival!"

"You have a ticket for the Hoober-Hustle Music Festival? I thought it sold out in seconds!" I said. I was so surprised that I forgot to talk like a butler for a second. I hoped my new grunting boss was not annoyed.

He *was* annoyed, but not about that.

"No, I do not have a ticket!" he grunted very deep, very fancy, and very annoyed. "I will not be in the audience! I will be on the stage! For I am THE GREAT WOLFGOOSE PIGWIG, the STAR of the music festival!"

Chapter 2

Very good, sir," I said. And I said it very calmly.

But I was very excited!

Wolfgoose Pigwig is not only the most famous opera singer in the world, he is also famous for being very, very fancy.

His music is fancy! His clothes are fancy! His wigs are fancy! So very, very fancy!

Finally, I would have my chance to butle

for someone who truly wanted things fancy! I could serve fancy tea from a fancy teapot into a fancy cup!

My lifelong dream was about to come true!

Wolfgoose Pigwig told me that his driver would pick me up in front of my apartment building in one hour.

He told me exactly what to wear: my fanciest tuxedo, my fanciest tie, and my fanciest cummerbund, which is that fancy thing that goes across your stomach.

"Very good, sir," I said, and I meant it. This is what a butler lives for!

Pigwig hung up without another word.

I had a lot to do to get ready, but first I called my mom!

"Mom, I got a job! The perfect job! I'm going to the HooberHustle Music Festival with—!"

"Oh, honey, I'm so proud of you!" she gushed. "You're going to be a hip-hop star at last!"

"Uh, no," I said. "I'm going to be a butler—"

"WHAT? Didn't Krystal Wombat call you? Wasn't she looking for a hot hip-hop hit record?"

"Well, yes," I admitted, "but I don't want to make hot records! I want to be a butler!"

"Not *that* again," groaned my mom. "Well, if you're not going to be a hip-hop star, why are you going to a music festival?"

"I'm going to be the butler for Wolf-goose Pigwig, the star of the festival!"

"This could be your big break, DJ! YOU could be the costar of the festival."

"But Mom, he doesn't need a costar!"

"You never know," said Mom. "Promise me you'll at least take your microphone."

"Mom, I—"

"PROMISE ME!"

I didn't have any more time to argue. I promised!

After saying goodbye to my mom, I put on my fanciest clothes and packed a small bag with butler stuff . . . and a microphone. (It was a birthday present from my mom.)

And then I ran out the door to wait for Pigwig's driver.

Chapter 3

When I got outside, the first thing I heard was hoofbeats. It sounded like a horse was coming down the road.

I hoped it wasn't my former boss, President Horse G. Horse! He might still be mad about what happened. (Remember the disasters and mess I mentioned?)

But it wasn't the president—it was a horsedrawn carriage! A very fancy, old-

timey carriage like the Queen of Wingland might have used two hundred years ago!

And it was being driven by a *different* old boss of mine, Countess Poodle-oo.

I was her butler back when she was rich, but she lost all her money (not my fault) and has been working as a driver lately.

Unfortunately, she never actually learned how to drive a car. And it did not look like she had ever learned how to drive a carriage, either!

The horse galloped wildly down the street! This made the carriage bounce, shudder, and bump into parked cars. Countess Poodle-oo could barely stay on the carriage, much less control it.

"WHOA!" she yelled. "Stop! Please, Baron Gustav, I am begging you! STOP!!!!"

The horse did stop, by crashing the carriage into my mailbox! (Now how was I going to get my copy of the *Butler News*?) But I was more worried about the Countess, who was nearly in tears.

"Countess? Are you OK?"

"Oh, DJ Funkyfoot, I am not hurt, but my new job is terrible!"

"No!" neighed the horse. "It is you who are terrible! You are a terrible carriage driver!"

"No!" shrieked the Countess. "It is YOU, Baron Gustav! You are a terrible . . . uh . . . carriage puller!"

"How dare you call me a carriage puller?" neighed the horse, and he slipped out of his harness, stood up on his hind legs, and went into a fighting stance!

Countess Poodle-oo jumped off the carriage and went into a fighting stance, too!

They circled each other, waving their hooves and paws in each other's faces.

"Oh, please don't fight!" I cried. But they did not listen to me.

But they DID listen to a very loud, very deep OINK from inside the carriage.

A tiny window opened and a pig's snout poked out.

"Oh, how tiresome! Oh, how very not fancy! Do I need to hire a new driver and a new horse?"

"No, sir!" cried Baron Gustav and Countess Poodle-oo. The Baron squirmed back into his harness. The Countess climbed back onto the roof of the carriage.

The pig snout grunted.

"Now . . . where is my new butler?" it demanded, in a very loud and very deep voice. It simply must have belonged to Wolfgoose Pigwig, my new boss!

"Here I am, sir," I said. "I am DJ Funky-foot, and I am at your service."

The pig snout poked a little farther out

of the window, and one piggy eye looked me up and down. Pigwig grunted.

"Well, you're NOT very fancy at all. But I need a butler and I need to leave town right away, so I guess you will have to do."

"I will work very hard to do everything you—"

"SHUSH! Did I not just say that I need to leave town RIGHT AWAY? I do not have time to sit in the street listening to a not-very-fancy butler talk all day long!"

"Very good, sir," I said.

The snout went back inside the carriage, and one tiny hoof came out and waved at Countess Poodle-oo.

"Drive on, driver! NOW!"

She did! And I had to run after the carriage as it careened through the city streets.

Interlude

uckily, I did not have to chase the carriage all the way out of town to the music festival.

After leaving a trail of dented cars, a bent flagpole, and five angry koalas, the carriage jolted to a stop outside of a familiar store: Koko Dodo's Cookie Shop!

"Oh, butler!" called Pigwig through the tiny window.

"Yes . . . sir . . . ?" I panted, out of breath from running so far.

"Step inside and purchase exactly seventeen New Zealand truffle-chip cookies from this shop. Have Koko send me the bill later, because we are in a hurry! So hurry!"

"Yes . . . sir!" Instead of catching my breath, I went straight into the store.

A dodo in a chef's hat stood behind the counter. It was my old friend, Koko Dodo.

"DJ Funkyfoot! Welcome!" he called.

"Huff . . . puff . . ." I replied.

"What are you telling me with the huff and the puff?" asked Koko. "Don't you want a cookie? We just pulled these yummy snickerdoodles out of the oven!"

"Hello, Koko!" I wheezed. "What I . . . really need is . . . seventeen New Zealand truffle-chip cookies."

"What are you telling me with seventeen cookies?" gasped Koko. "I bake cookies by the dozen. That's twelve! Not seventeen!"

Even though I had only been working for Wolfgoose Pigwig for ten minutes, I was pretty sure he would NOT be happy with only twelve cookies.

"How long would it take to bake

more?" I asked, looking at my watch. I was running out of time!

"It cannot be done," wailed Koko. "I have no more New Zealand truffles! The three baby chicks just ate them!"

I looked over and saw three baby chicks sitting on chairs around a table with an empty truffle jar on it.

"Oh no! I'm doomed!" I said.

"Me too," said Koko Dodo, "because those chicks are going to start pooping on my chairs now!"

Just then, a duck came out of the kitchen with a tray of cookies.

"Greetings, your Royal Highness," I exclaimed, bowing.

"Greetings, DJ Funkyfoot," said the duck, who is Koko's helper and also the Queen of Wingland. "Don't worry! I know what to do!"

"You do?" I asked hopefully.

"Yes, we're going to make the baby chicks wear diapers from now on."

"Oh," I said. "I thought you meant you knew what to do about the cookies."

"Oh yes," she said. "I can solve that, too. I have just baked a batch of Australian truffle-chip cookies. I'll put five Australian truffle-chip cookies in the bottom of the bag, then the twelve New Zealand truffle-chip cookies on top. No one will ever notice!"

"Wonderful! Thank you so very much, your Royal Highness!" I said, taking the bag. "And thank you, Koko! Please send the bill to Wolfgoose Pigwig!"

As I turned to run out of the store, I noticed Koko and the Queen looking worried. But I didn't have time to find out why.

I ran out of the store, handed the bag of cookies through the window to Wolfgoose Pigwig, and jumped onto the roof of the carriage beside the Countess before she drove away!

PART 2

To Serve a Star

Chapter 4

was very happy! My new boss was very picky, but I had worked hard and everything had worked out just fine.

"STOP THE CARRIAGE!" roared a very loud, very low, very angry voice.

The Countess and the Baron were so startled that they stopped the carriage in the middle of the street without even arguing with each other.

The door opened.

The bag of cookies was thrown into the street.

And then, out stepped Wolfgoose Pigwig.

He looked like the greatest opera star in the world, which he was. He was dressed like a king. He wore a monocle and a wig with so many curls and ribbons that it made him seem almost twice as tall as he was.

He stamped on the bag of cookies with one hoof. Then the other hoof. Then he began jumping up and down and stomping on it with all four hooves at once! His monocle went flying. His cravat went flying. His wig went flying.

In fact, ALL of his clothes went flying.

All around us, traffic screeched to a halt as chickens, chipmunks, and a tour bus

full of church mice all stopped to stare at the sight of a naked pig jumping up and down on a bag of cookies.

I scrambled to pick up the clothing and wiggery.

"Sir! Is there a problem, sir?" I asked, almost keeping calm.

"Of course there is a problem, butler! Can't you smell it?"

I sniffed. Being a dog, I have a very

strong sense of smell. All I could smell was angry pig and smooshed truffle cookies.

"I do not smell a problem, sir," I said.

"Well, I do," he squealed, his very low voice getting very high again for just a second. "I smell twelve New Zealand truffle-chip cookies and five—*sniff*—Australian."

"Oh, I am so sorry, sir," I said. "I was not aware that there was a big difference."

"A real butler would," he said. "Alas, I fear you are not a very good butler."

I gasped! I almost started to cry, but butlers do not cry on the job!

"And now you stand there almost crying. What a bad butler! You're fired!"

My beautiful dream of being a fancy butler for a fancy boss had come true, but

it was already over! No! I couldn't let that happen!

"Please, Sir Pigwig! Give me another chance," I begged.

"Well, OK, but only because I don't have time to hire a better butler."

As I helped Pigwig get dressed and climb back into the carriage, I made up my mind: I would be a better butler. In fact, I would be the BEST butler!

Chapter 5

got my chance just a minute later.

"Stop the carriage!" Sir Pigwig yelled as we went past Nedra Gnu's Coffee Cafe. "Butler, get me a triple-whip hazelnut drip express espresso, with a dollop of hand-whipped cream."

"Yes, sir!" I replied and trotted into the cafe. This time, I thought, I would show him my true butler skills! I would have preferred to serve some tea, of course, but this coffee sounded pretty fancy!

It was fancy! It took Nedra Gnu a lot of work to make that one cup of coffee come pouring out of a very loud machine.

"Careful," said Nedra, as she handed me the cup. "It's very, very, very, very hot."

I trotted back to the carriage and handed the coffee through the tiny window.

"Your coffee, sir!"

I heard a sniff, a snuffle, and a slurp.

Then the cup of coffee came flying out of the tiny window. It splattered on the ground and got very, very, very, very HOT coffee all over my suit.

"Do you call that a dollop? That was, at most, a smidgen," he grumbled. "Alas,

I fear you are not a very good butler. You are fired again!"

"Please, sir! Give me another chance!"

He did.

This time it was to get him a new fluffy cushion for his carriage seat.

But the cushion I found at Hank's Cushion Depot was TOO fluffy! I tried to defluff it and got bits of fluff all over my suit.

Then he asked for a tuba. But the one I found wasn't tubular enough.

Then he asked for a record player. But the only one I could find had two turntables and he only wanted one.

Then he wanted a record of the Wingland Symphony Orchestra playing *Pigletto*. I actually found that, but he listened to it and complained that the flute section was out of tune.

Then he asked for a ballpoint pen that wrote with purple ink, a chess set where all the pieces were little horsies, a plumb bob, wig powder, tail polish, snout cream, pickle relish, a ship in a bottle, and an ice-cream cone with one scoop of every flavor, except mint chocolate chip.

We drove all over the city, and I ran in and out of dozens of shops, stores, and flea markets, trying to find it all.

And I did!

BUT...

The pen wrote in the wrong shade of purple.

The chess horsies looked too much like Baron Gustav.

The plumb bob bobbed too much.

The wig powder was too powdery.

The tail polish was the wrong shade.

The snout cream was for wild boars, not domesticated hogs, and he, Wolfgoose Pigwig, was certainly NOT a wild boar.

The pickle relish was not Cousin Yuk Yuk brand.

The ship in the bottle was not historically accurate.

And lastly, he changed his mind and decided he DID want mint chocolate chip after all, but not on top, he wanted it added to the middle, and that resulted in the huge stack of ice cream tipping over and all the flavors landing on my head and making a huge sticky mess of my suit, my tie, and, yes, even my cummerbund!

Chapter 6

P igwig was just about to send me back to get another ice-cream cone when Countess Poodle-oo spoke up.

"Excuse me, sir, but it is getting late! If we don't start galloping out of the city right now we will never get to the concert on time."

"Is there time for me to hire a better driver, a better horse, and a better butler?"

"No, sir," she said, wiping away a tear.

"Alas!" said Pigwig. "After the concert, I will fire all of you. But for now, away we go! Off to the HooberHustle Musical Festival! Huzzah!!!"

He slammed his tiny window shut.

I was so covered in cushion fluff, coffee stains, and sticky, melting ice cream that the Countess and the Baron had to help me climb up on the roof.

We were all sniffling and trying not to cry about losing our jobs.

"Maybe if we do a really great job for the rest of the day, he'll change his mind," said the Baron.

"Oh, I hope so!" said the Countess.

I hoped so, too! Even though this dream job was more like a nightmare job, it was still a job! And it might be my last chance to butle. Who would hire me after this?

Interlude

The Baron and the Countess agreed to stop fighting and start driving the carriage properly.

Soon we were speeding toward the festival, which is held every year in a farmer's field about twenty miles out of town.

Of course, when I say we were speeding, I mean we were going pretty fast for a horse-drawn carriage. We were NOT going pretty fast for a car. In fact, all the cars were passing us. So were trucks, buses, motorcycles, and a big, beautiful double-decker food van.

On the side of the van, it said PENGUINI'S PORTABLE PIZZERIA!

As it drove past the carriage, it slowed down, and Penguini himself yelled to us from the window.

"Hey! Mr. Funkyfoot, my good friend! I'm so happy to see you!"

"Hello, Penguini. I am always happy to see you, but actually right now I am very sad. We are all going to lose our jobs after the music festival."

"Oh, Mr. Funkyfoot, I am so sorry to hear that! I can't help you keep your job, but I can cheer you up! Come find my van during the festival, and I will make you all something special!"

That did make us all feel a little better, and we waved at Penguini's food van as it sped off into the distance.

PART 3
Highway Snobbery

Chapter 7

P retty soon, all the traffic headed to the music festival had passed us, and we were alone on the highway.

We were going SO SLOW! And then we started going up a long hill and went EVEN SLOWER!

Pigwig stuck his snout out the window and began hollering at the Baron.

"Can't you go any faster?"

By now the poor horse was huffing and

puffing as bad as I had been earlier. He couldn't even answer.

"RUDE!" grunted Pigwig. "How about you, Countess? Can't you make him go any faster?"

"No, I can't," she said. "But we are almost to the top of the hill. Once we start going downhill, we'll go much faster."

"HMMPH!" snuffled Pigwig. "Well, we had better! My many fans are waiting for me at the festival!"

But when we reached the top of the hill, the Baron didn't go faster. He stopped.

"WHAT NOW?" grunted Pigwig.

The Baron was still trying to catch his breath, so I answered for him.

"Sir, the Baron has stopped because there is a tree blocking the way."

"A tree? What is a tree doing in the middle of the road?"

"He appears to be robbing us, sir."

Pigwig let out a wild oink that was both very deep and very high at the same time. And definitely very loud. Then he leaped out of the carriage.

"What is the meaning of this, tree?"

"Allow me to introduce myself," said the tree, who was wearing a pointy green hat with a feather in it. "My name is

Sherwood Forest! I rob from the rich and give to the poor. So please, hand over all your money!"

"What if I don't?" snorted Pigwig.

"Then I'll fall over on you, pin you to the ground, and play songs on my lute until you do!!!"

"You wouldn't dare!"

Sherwood pulled a lute out of his leaves and began to play a merry tune with his branches.

And then he sang.

"Hey nonny, nonny, let's all dance a jig, while I fall over on this fancy pig!"

"EGAD!" bellowed Pigwig. "Your singing is terrible! But my servants will put a stop to it. Driver! Horse! Butler! Attack!!!"

But the Countess and the Baron were busy dancing a jig . . . and falling in love. The last I saw them, they were skipping down the hill, hoof in paw. (I was later invited to their wedding, but that's a different story.)

Chapter 8

Well, butler, that leaves you to deal with this. Attack that tree!"

I didn't know what to do. I wanted do a good job so that Pigwig wouldn't fire me. But how could I do a good job of attacking a tree? There's only one thing a dog can do to a tree and . . . Well, that's just not something a butler would do!

But what *would* a butler do?

If I could figure out what a butler would do and then do it, I could prove that I was a good butler!

The first thing a butler does is stay calm, so I started there.

"Sir," I said, calmly, "I am unable to stop the tree from taking your money. But once he does, I will help you carry on. I will work hard to get you to the music festival and get you ready to perform."

Before Pigwig could answer, Sherwood Forest took out his lute again and began to play and sing.

"Hey diddly diddly, tra la la la, fa fa, I think you better listen to the smart Chihuahua."

"Enough!" squealed Pigwig. "I can take no more of your singing! Here's my money!"

He pulled out a bag full of gold.

"Thanks!" said Sherwood Forest. "I know a family of mushrooms that can really use this!"

Sherwood Forest grabbed the gold, laid down on his side, and rolled down the hill and out of sight.

Chapter 9

A ll right, butler," said Pigwig. "Here's your chance. How are you going to get me to the festival when we don't have a driver or a horse? The carriage isn't going to drive itself!"

"Actually, sir," I said, "if you take a close look at the carriage, you will notice that it is indeed driving itself."

The carriage was in fact beginning to

roll forward and down the hill toward the music festival.

"My wigs are in there!" yelled Pigwig as he jumped inside.

What could I do? I had promised to help him get to the festival! So I jumped in, too.

The added weight of myself and the pig made the carriage roll faster. And soon the hill got steeper, and it went even faster. In seconds, we were speeding out of control!

"We're finally making some progress," said Pigwig, looking out his tiny window as the countryside flashed past. "Now we can stop for dinner before we get to the festival."

"I'm afraid not, sir," I said calmly.

"Not enough time?" asked Pigwig.

"It is not so much the time, sir," I said, still calmly, "as it is the fact that we cannot stop at all. Nor can we steer. We are, in fact, doomed to ride this carriage until it crashes into something."

"Well, I hope it crashes into a fancy restaurant," said Pigwig. "I simply cannot perform on an empty stomach!"

Luckily, the carriage was slowing down! Unluckily, the angry mob of gatekeepers, ticket-takers, and Barnyard String Quartet members was catching up to us.

Finally, with a small thud, we ran into a large van and stopped.

Thud.

"Was that a fancy restaurant?" asked Pigwig hopefully.

I looked out the window. Penguini was waving at us from the door of his double-decker food van.

"Yes, sir," I said. "It's a very fancy restaurant."

"It had better be," grumbled Pigwig.

GRAND FINALE

Ready, Steady, Snore!

Chapter 10

O nce the angry mob found out that the carriage belonged to Pigwig, they stopped being angry.

They cheered as he stepped out of the carriage and into Penguini's Portable Pizzeria.

"Welcome, Mr. Funkyfoot," called Penguini. "And welcome to you, Sir Pigwig! I will be honored to cook for you!"

"I only eat the fanciest, finest foods," Pigwig sniffed.

"I only serve the fanciest, finest foods," replied Penguini.

"Hmm," grunted Pigwig. "We shall see. Bring me one of everything."

Wolfgoose Pigwig must be the pickiest pig in the world, but Penguini was more than a match for him!

"How do you like the spaghetti with slop sauce?" asked Penguini.

"Fantastic!" oinked Pigwig.

"The slop-stuffed manicotti?"

"Magnificent!"

"My famous five-slop ravioli?"

"Delicious!"

"The ziti with slop scampi? My mother's recipe."

"Wonderful!"

"How about the gnocchi ala sloppitini?"

"Scrumptious!"

"The slop parmagiana?"

"Stupendous!"

"And lastly, an extra-large scoop of slop-ripple gelato?"

"PERFECTION!" oinked Pigwig, deep and loud.

"Ah, thank you, Sir Pigwig!"

"I don't have any money to pay for this," squeaked Pigwig, high and whispery.

"Money? No, no, no! I do not want money from the greatest opera singer in the world! I want only music! I want to hear your beautiful voice singing my favorite opera, *Pigletto*!"

"In that case, box up a pizza with extra slop sauce to go! Butler! We must get to the stage! Penguini and my many, many, many fans await!"

Chapter 11

Soon we were backstage, waiting for the curtain to rise.

"Greetings, Mr. Funkyfoot," said a very polite voice.

It was Cedric Dragonsmasher, the butler to the President of the United States.

"Greetings, Mr. Dragonsmasher," I said politely. "I did not expect to see you at a music festival."

"My boss, President Horse, wanted

to come to the concert tonight," he explained. "But his mom sent him to bed early, because he had tracked mud into the White House again. So I have come with this machine to record it for him."

He was about to show me the machine when a loud and angry oink interrupted us.

"Butler! Stop the chitter-chatter and help me get ready!"

"Yes, sir! Very sorry, sir!" I replied.

I wiped slop sauce off of Pigwig's clothes.

I sprinkled fresh wig powder on his wig.

I combed and curled his tail.

I shined his snout, polished his hooves, and unwaxed his ears.

Then I set up the record player with Pigwig's *Pigletto* music and hooked it up to the festival's big speakers.

"All is ready, sir."

"Very good," he said. "I have to admit that you have done a good job today. You got me and my wigs here on time. You found the perfect place to have the perfect meal, despite everything. And you remained calm and polite through it all. You are a very good butler."

"Oh, thank you so much, sir!" I said, almost forgetting to remain calm.

"However," he continued, "you are still fired."

This time I did forget to stay calm.

"WHAT? WHY?"

"Just look at yourself! You're a mess! You're covered in slop sauce, hoof polish, coffee stains, melted ice cream, pickle relish, pillow fluff, tree leaves, and . . . are those cello chunks?"

"Yes, sir, from when the carriage ran over the Barnyard String Quartet's instruments."

"Well, it's very unfancy. And it will not do. No, it will not do at all. Tomorrow, I will find a new butler. But today, you are fired."

"Yes, sir," I sniffled.

"And now," continued Pigwig, "I feel so full from that meal that I think I'll lay down and have a little nap."

"But sir, it's time to start the show!"

"Did you say 'start the show'?" yelled the stage manager, a rather pushy walrus. "OK! Start the show, everybody! Start the music! Open the curtain! Turn on the lights!"

The music started!

The curtain opened!

The lights turned on!

Chapter 12

n the center of the stage, in the center of the spotlight, was a sleeping pig.

ZZZZZZZZZZZZ! snored the pig with a voice that was both deep and loud.

Also in the spotlight was . . . me!

I froze!

ZZZZZZZ! came another snore.

I didn't know what to do.

ZZZZZZZZ!

"Why isn't he singing?" yelled a confused donkey in the audience.

ZZZZZZ!

"Wake him up!" yelled an impatient lily.

ZZZZZ!

"I PAID MONEY! I WANT TO HEAR A PIG SING!!!!" roared an angry yak.

ZZZZZ!

"BOOOOOOOOO!" yelled the entire audience at once!

But by now I had realized something.

Pigwig's snoring was quite musical! And it kept up a steady beat.

It was like . . . the bass line of a hip-hop song.

A very tall turtle in the audience threw his shoe at Pigwig. It missed and hit the record player. SCRRAATCH!

It was like . . . the record-scratching in a hip-hop song.

And then a tiny, adorable shrub in the audience yelled, "Hey everybody! Stop booing and listen!"

It was ShrubBaby, the chaotic but adorable baby shrub who was once my boss for one chaotic but adorable day.

"That's DJ MC Funkyfoot!" she hollered.

"The hip-hop star?" asked the whole audience.

"No," I said. "I'm not a hip-hop star. I'm a—"

"We can't hear you!" yelled the audience. "Could you please use a microphone?"

I looked around but didn't see a microphone. And then I remembered the promise I had made to my mom. I reached into my pocket and pulled out my microphone.

The crowd cheered.

"I'm sorry," I said. "ShrubBaby is adorable, but she's incorrect. I'm not a hip-hop star."

"BUT YOU COULD BE!" yelled Shrub-Baby.

"YOU BETTER BE," yelled the entire audience, "or we're going to throw a fit and tear down the stage and roll around in the mud and say bad words and—"

But I wasn't listening.

I was stepping over to the record player.

Chapter 13

scratched the record in time to Pigwig's bass beat.

Scritchy scritchy ZZZZZZZ

Scritchy scritchy ZZZZZZZ

Scrit scrit scritty scrit ZZZZZZZ

"Now rap!" the adorable baby shrub was yelling.

"Yes, ShrubBaby," I said. And then I rapped:

This is DJ Funkyfoot
At your service
I have to admit
I am a little nervous . . .

Yeah, I had rap lessons
from an early age.
But this is the first time
I've ever been on stage.

Dad said be a DJ,
Mom said be an MC.
But as for me,
I just want to serve tea.

Hot tea, iced tea,
Black tea, green tea,
Anyway you like it,
It's all the same to me.

But those who hire me,
Never want to drink the tea.
Instead they cause trouble
from here to infinity.

Poodle and shrub,
Horse and hog . . .
It's been a wild ride
For such a small dog.

I got ice cream in my hair
And spaghetti on my pants . . .
But enough about me,
Now it's your turn to dance!

SKRITCHHY SKRITTCHY ZZZ ZZZ ZZZZZ

Butlers should never brag. But I have to be honest. The crowd seemed to like it. They danced. They sang along. They waved their arms in the air like they just didn't care.

Then they made me do it again. And again! And again!!!

Luckily, Pigwig just kept snoring that wonderful, deep, fancy snore.

Epilogue

I will have to make this short, because my new boss wants a cup of tea.

The crowd quite enjoyed my little performance. And so did Krystal Wombat, the president of Wombat Jam Records, when she heard Cedric Dragonsmasher's recording of it.

"This is the hot hip-hop hit record I've been waiting for!" she insisted.

Well, a good butler doesn't argue if he can help it, so I agreed to let her release it.

And she was right.

For some reason—which I admit I cannot possibly understand—it was hot. REALLY HOT! Hot as a cup of tea that hasn't cooled off enough to be served.

Radio stations played it. Teenage plants and animals downloaded it. Cousin Yuk Yuk paid to use it in a pickle relish commercial. (I changed the words to be about pickles instead of tea.)

It made millions of dollars.

Of course, I had to split half of that with Sir Pigwig. After all, it's his snoring that gives the record its beat.

And I bought ShrubBaby a ShrubBuggy. And then I bought the Countess and the

Baron a fancy new carriage as a wedding present.

But I still have way too much money left over, even after donating a lot to charity.

"DJ, you've got enough money to hire your OWN butler," ShrubBaby told me.

And then I remembered that I still needed a job . . .

So I hired myself to be my own butler.

Finally, I have a good boss.

Now, if you'll excuse me, I need to go make myself a cup of tea.

ABOUT THE
AUTHOR AND ILLUSTRATOR

TOM ANGLEBERGER is the *New York Times* bestselling author of the Origami Yoda series, as well as many other books for kids. He created DJ Funkyfoot, a Chihuahua butler, with his wife, Cece Bell, for the Inspector Flytrap series. In real life, Tom and Cece do have a Chihuahua, but he's more of a biter than a butler. Visit Tom at origamiyoda.com.

HEATHER FOX is an illustrator of stories for children. When she isn't creating, she's probably drinking a hot cup of coffee, eating Chinese food, or chasing down her dog, Sir Hugo, who has stolen one of her socks. She lives in Lancaster, Pennsylvania, with her husband (and author!) Jonathan Stutzman.